I0522668

# MYTHICAL PLACES

JESSICA HOLLANDER

Sonder Press
New York
www.thesonderpress.com



ISBN 978-0-9997501-8-6

Cover Design: Chad Miller

First U.S. edition 2020
Printed in the USA
Distribution via Ingram

# Acknowledgments

I'd like to thank Sonder Press and Elena Stiehler for the incredible support and editing expertise. Thanks to *Sonora Review* and *Potomac Review* for publishing previous versions of "Nebraska" and "Home" respectively. Thanks to the University of Nebraska at Kearney for giving me a home, a place to play, and a place to teach so many wonderful students. Thank you to my parents Tom and Cindy Hollander and my brother Daniel Hollander for always listening. And thanks to Richard Mocarski and my kids Oliver, Chloe, and Allegra for the endless fun, trouble, and inspiration.

for my Nebraska kids, Oliver, Chloe, and Allegra

# CONTENTS

# NEBRASKA

LIKE HERMIT CRABS SCATTERING from shell to shell, the young mother's family moves to Nebraska. Goodbye ocean, sand, Mom, Dad. When her husband offered the country's stomach alongside a tripled salary, the young mother said *Why not?* Yellow-brown landscape beneath a gray sky. Chain-linked fences, American flags, train tracks. Big water traded for big land, perhaps a place she can stand without sinking. They move late fall when the world seems to be crumbling. For her son's sake the young mother points out Sandhill cranes in dried cornfields, gray birds with long legs and necks and red-splotched heads. She turns to see Clint asleep in his car seat. "Looking for bugs," her husband says. She has spent weeks packing boxes, hauling bags for Purple Heart pick-up, saying goodbye to her family and her husband's family, all of whom several times wetted Clint's head. Driving east feels like floating. "They're elegant hunters," the young mother says. She has read up on this place, knows a festival is dedicated to these birds in spring. The cranes peck the ground like survival is easy. The young mother is excited to see something new.

The young mother had not minded work at the newspaper. Stacks of drafts, the keyboard sticky from dripped tea, post-its stuck to her corkboard wall—the landscape of her dim, warm cube wasn't why she'd quit copyediting. "Should I negotiate some work for you?" her husband had asked. It was a big position in Nebraska he would move into. They ate bagels and berries, one of their last San Diego breakfasts. Wet wind blew from the open balcony and she filled her lungs, the salt air novel now that she was once again leaving. "What about Clint?" the young mother asked, wiping his blue-stained cheeks. She'd researched ways motherhood infects ambition, how the more kids a woman has the less invested she becomes elsewhere. She'd meant to write a piece about it. "He's survived two years with grandmas watching him," her husband said. "We'll find a daycare with grandmas." She hated the phrase *career path*. Paths are like ladders like mountains like plot arcs. Why should she pack her life into a parabola? "No," she said, and her son grinned at the word with mischief. "He can stay home with me. It's the space I need. I want to write."

Here is the middle of the country, where all things crossing must pass. Now driving beneath an archway anchored with winged horses signals home. The young mother has read about this Great Platte Archway: three hundred feet straddling the interstate, its red-orange-yellow resembling a Nebraska sunset. Inside, Westward Expansion is presented in an extravagant multimedia display, already once bankrupt and revived. She is not prepared for the silver horses, one at each end of the arch, posed mid-leap. The metal wings are three times the horses' size and not attached to their backs but buttressed above and away from them, an artist's vision of dimensionality. The feathers spread and flutter out like blades. Maybe they aren't wings but something pursuing the horses, clawing at their backs. The horses are escaping. They leap from either end of the archway, fleeing history.

The young mother wonders if new shells feel different to hermit crabs; if they miss their old shells. She hasn't written since grad school, her first move to an unfamiliar landscape. Thick-shouldered mountains and snow pocked roads. She'd published features in national magazines; her program had spotlighted her on their webpage. A young talent. A scuttling star. An impulse to grow larger is what makes crabs search for new shells. While she wrote, her husband worked diligently, refused to ski, missed his family, and when she got pregnant—not on purpose but not the end of the world—she quietly followed him home, crammed herself back into her old San Diego life. But she found she couldn't write anymore. It was the opposite of writer's block: ideas leaking constantly into the ocean before she could jot them down. Or so it seemed. The baby grew impossibly big; her stomach stretched along with it, as she watched the stories swim away. Once she had written here, when she was young and fit this shoreline.

The young mother is like a balloon tied to a bumper, along for the ride. She believes not owning a house will prolong this feeling of suspension. She decorates their rented walls, buys a turkey, waves to neighbors in purple and gray coats like they're part of a painting she's stepped into. The air's cold but her husband smiles as though she's a different person or a person she once was and dug up again. This energy. On the phone, her mother warns, "Beware happiness triggered by change. And holidays." With so much to do she has no time to write. Thanksgiving belongs to the stomach. She stuffs turkey, her husband fills pies. Clint digs dough and nudges cranberries; the young mother admires him. Motherhood gives an excuse to excuse oneself from the world briefly. Holding Clint's sticky hand, peering through the lit oven door and pointing, she thinks *why not have another?*

"What do I *do?*" The young mother repeats the question, to her husband's assistant, the woman at the museum, a bagger loading groceries into her trunk. She has learned to cook well. She folds laundry quickly. Her legs and back have grown accustomed to floor-sitting. It is a question of self-worth, though she *knows* it takes stamina and intelligence to raise a child well. She is a journalist, too. "I *think,*" she tells the assistant, the bagger, her parents who call late night whispering. "I interpret the world." Soon, soon. Soon she'll populate it with better questions.

Do hermit crabs remember a watery childhood? High school summers on the Pacific Beach boardwalk, the young mother sold ice cream cones from a shack in a line of shacks with colorful signs. She came to know her husband when Sundays he ordered so many cones she had to help carry them, snug in cardboard carriers, down to the beach where his family would patchwork enough towels together to form their own island. Never a cousin or parent accompanied him, though they would have. He stood tallest at both their high schools; he played sports because they begged him. He was an expert on the debate team. One afternoon with burnt shoulders he called himself a lobster and squeezed his hands like claws. "I like the meat in lobsters," she said. "Just not prying them open." She had won a senior writing award, and looking up at him she felt worthy. "You've got to cook them right," he said. She walked barefoot, the warm sand always a shock she wanted to sink into. A claw latched onto hers and softened to a hand. Water washed up the edge of the world, and she swelled.

Above sales fliers in the grocery's wind-swept entry, a tack board advertises church potlucks, consignment sales, childcare. Clint spins a small steering wheel in a shopping cart resembling a green truck cab while the young mother reads a flier: *Calling All Aspiring Authors Join Kearney Writers Group!* underscored with typewriter clipart and a dialogue bubble from a stern Shakespeare head saying *Serious Writers Only*. She considers the telephone tabs but assumes they mean fiction, and it's not fiction she's after. Clint squirms in his seat. Outside, the roads dusted with snow look blurry. Beneath their hung paintings, the walls of their rental home belong to someone else. Even these grocery shelves with strange products among familiar ones—everything seems borrowed from another person's life, like it isn't only a new shell she has moved to but a new ocean. She pushes through the store, debates apples or applesauce, considers yogurt, asks Clint, "What sounds good to you?" But her voice is watery in a way she thinks the landscape isn't the problem, more like the prying loose from old shells has made her soft parts peak oddly, with the stickiest bits left behind.

Her parents come for Christmas. They admire the garlands, the blue-green Christmas tree strung with tinsel, Clint's new haircut. "How you holding up?"

her father asks. She thinks of steel beams beneath skin, propping bones. Her computer in the corner sits dusty. Besides trips to the grocery and craft shop, most of the time she stays inside on the carpet with Clint, driving cars, inching a wooden puzzle together. "Well, it's Christmas," she says. "There's presents to wrap." Her mom eyes her stomach. "Why don't you buy a house? Act like you're going to stay awhile." The young mother crosses her ankles, blankets her legs. She has gained weight but is not pregnant. Clint shows Grandpa his new fire truck. "See?" he says. The firemen cannot turn their heads. They must bring water from a yellow string. "I don't have the energy," she tells her mother. She watches her son. "Play," he tells her, and she does.

The young mother tracks her monthly cycle, decides when best to have sex. She initiates with her husband in the morning, when it's easy. Afterward, the bedroom bathed in shades of purple looks bruised, dark near their bed, the windows violet with morning light. "Maybe we should join a church," her husband says. "Not for God. For community." They lay naked waist down with sleep shirts twisted. Hot air blows from the floor vent; her skin has dried and cracked from the false heat. "We had community," the young mother says, wishing he'd leave her this peace. "We fled." Clint snores softly from the monitor, a constant presence. Her husband's family has not yet visited; they claim inability to separate from their ocean. "It's my fault this time," he says, putting his arm around her like she's the one who needs comforting. "I should've tried getting you a job." She grows warm beneath him. Her skin hurts less. "Clint's still too young," she says. She didn't want a job. The plan was to write.

For two years they'd returned to college jobs, ate dinner at her parents' on Saturday, his on Sunday, but their parents' questions stacked up, equated to the same thing: when will you make more, buy a house, a new car, move up? Their cracked-wall apartment was high enough to see the ocean. The young mother took up knitting, sat cross-legged on the cement balcony stained by dashed cigarettes and covered her growing belly with weave while white boats sailed. Evenings, she and her husband walked to the beach feeling starved of water and sand only to return to their apartment complaining—it stuck in their teeth, between toes: this grit. The landscape heaped on their skin. When the baby was born their apartment crammed with bouncers, swings, strollers, blankets, hats, poop, drool. Beneath them was a chiropractor, a tanning salon, a raw juice shop. Beside them were beach bums staining hallways with wet feet, rubbing the carpet raw with boards. Too much clutter to write. On the balcony with the baby, the ocean spread like a swelled threat. Sand collected constantly in Clint's diaper, in every fold of his fat little body.

Though it is mid-winter now, the young mother takes up running. She could spend this time reading, thinking, studying, writing; but in the still-dark bedroom she pulls on long underwear, sweats, scarf, and headband, needing to wrestle her body into a shape different from this one. Beyond her neighborhood, shadowed fields show endless room to expand. She jogs through crisp air piercing her cheeks until her lungs burn sufficiently and she knows her muscles will all day remember the ache. When she arrives home reddened, Clint and her husband play on the carpet with blocks and wooden animals on high towers. "Mama!" they call. Still in pajamas, they smile as she stretches her pained muscles beside them. The warmth of the duplex thaws her skin while splitting it. "Cold hands," Clint says, climbing into her lap. "It's a circus," her husband says, adding a rhino to the stack. "They're smiling."

A workday is the easiest answer, clocked in, clocked out, the satisfaction of minutes. But work is not the answer. But she could volunteer somewhere. She could research oceans, hermit crabs, digestion, send her features to be published. But her husband says when she is ready, or never, I don't mind as long as you're happy. But raising children is a contribution. But she doesn't expect to be happy. But is that a requirement?

The young mother sits at her computer while Clint naps. She views pictures of hermit crabs beneath bruised shells, on red legs, crossing pebbly sand. If only she had an article to show, even a few words on a blank page, but it's been too long to find the right note. She isn't alone in this—people get stuck; they run hands along walls searching. She once was a talent, skittering towards new heights. "What do I *do*?" In her living room she repeats the question. Action equates to living; doing is working, the only way to define identity. "I've taken up running. I'm getting in shape." Something fetus-like about the ones outside their shells. She understands her parents' argument: if she is only a mother, there could be a divorce. No work history, no portfolio, no income. But she can imagine herself poor, living in a shack in some warm woods, growing her own food, getting by minimally. Clint could have the bed; she would take the floor. She is training her body for something.

The young mother runs through neighborhoods near theirs but not theirs. She tries to know this landscape, imagines lives through parted curtains, guesses crops grown in frosted fields—corn, soybeans, corn—this world could be hers. There are neighbors, parent associations, soil ripe for gardening. Come spring, the sky will fill with Sandhill cranes come to hunt these fields in the midst of migrating elsewhere, and the young mother could be here watching. Back in the warm duplex, she sees her face flush in the mirror and believes herself haunted. "How many miles? How fast?" her husband asks. The young mother shrugs. "Until I want to stop." Her husband pats his stomach, a slight pouch. Her stomach has flattened like the landscape. "Maybe I'll start running," he says. "Why don't you clean and cook, too?" asks the young mother. There's so little that belongs to her. But running makes her pliable. Aggravation seeps so far in she almost forgets she lives beside it. She feels serene cooking oatmeal while her husband showers; she likes the smell of him coming into the kitchen, clean beside her, how he hugs her despite her sweat stains. The country's middle isn't respected like the edges but it holds the whole together. Clint scoops oatmeal so bits fall to the table. She's surrounded, protected. She lives in a stomach, ready to expand. She touches the edges of her country, tries to trust they won't sink or burn or fray.

# HOME



WEDNESDAY NIGHTS THE FLIES came. Wiggled through the old screens, knocked drunkenly around the kitchen, settled on the trashcan overloaded with diapers and dinner scraps. Wails came from the train yard like the air was haunted. Amee stood by the small stove light, batting flies and eating cheese as she cut it. The windows were dark. She saw the streetlight but not the men. The basketball hit the drive, rim, backdrop, puncturing the ghostly moans. She and Joe had moved to the neighborhood two months ago, the same week as William, with his story worse than theirs. He provided escape from diaper loads, milk stains, scrubbed fingernails, piercing squawks in the dead night—an infant was an animal. William had eyed her and Joe, slumped on the couch, like he knew who they'd be in ten years: ironic, divorced, twenty pounds overweight.

Nine minutes since Laurelee last cried. Easier to think of her sweet pink face without the panic that came from calming her, because the doctor had said babies sense stress, looking directly at Amee while he said it, and now she wouldn't let the baby see her face when she cried. Which Joe said was crazy but what could she do? She couldn't change her face. Her own mother had propped bottles against pillows, sores spreading across Amee's mouth for a week before her mother had gotten the infection treated. A litany of sins she had admitted after Amee had Lauralee. Parents were given babies like pets, no tests, no practice. Anyone with ten months to spare could bring one home.

The ball's beats slowed, then ceased. Only the moaning remained: big, dumb animals being tortured. The flies came alongside the half-dead cows filling the train that stopped here overnight for some reason. Amee cut up an orange thinking she'd leave half for Joe, then sat at the table and ate his pieces slowly. The first couple weeks she'd invited William inside, but he didn't know when to leave and she didn't like to be known as a bitch. She and Joe named the driveway the limit.

The screen door opened and Joe said, "Sky's purple. Come see."

"He still out there?"

"Yep."

She didn't worry about Joe here. He didn't drink or lock himself in rooms. He was from this small Nebraskan town, had lived with his parents and brothers in this house that had been cemented to the ground for a hundred and forty years, on this street with no sirens or glass breaking, no people screaming at each other, no gunshots. The women who'd lived here and given birth here: Amee sometimes imagined she was them, walking from room to room while Joe went interviewing. The house was big enough that those early women must've been rich, with husbands who owned half the town in crops or were early investors who thought *why wouldn't people want to live in the middle of nowhere Nebraska?*

Joe thought she minded but she didn't. In some part of her brain lay things she cared about besides the house and baby—she'd planned to get a doctorate, conduct studies, own mice—but they wouldn't come into focus. She needed a microscope, a scientific manual. Someday she'd tweeze out these old ambitions and trap them between glass, slide them under a light, or else serenely lose them in the cracks.

She followed Joe outside. William sat on the lawn leaning with his elbow on one knee, his big shoulders uneven. Why he'd moved to this neighborhood of paint-peeled houses and popped-up weeds, all shedding and blemishes—he'd come from the west-side mansions—she didn't know. He wore a T-shirt and basketball shorts. He must have come home and put these things on and waited for Joe to take out the trash. It was too dark to see his face.

"We'll hear her," Joe told Amee, sitting by William. "You have to come out this far."

Amee stayed on the porch. She saw where they were looking. "It's the lights from the amphitheater." She'd read about it opening this weekend with a local country band. Now that she was listening, she heard human crooning alongside the animals' moans.

"The sky's full of bruises," William said. He had a potbelly bigger than the basketball. He had two teenage kids. "It's a punch in the stomach."

"The place I told Amee about isn't here anymore," Joe said. "You could hear the corn grow."

"Corn doesn't grow now," William said. "It shoots from the ground like bullets, more machine than plant."

A train whistled and roared for a long minute like music from another dimension. Its alien whine, its layers of echoes, obliterated the crooning.

"I like the trains here," Amee said. "They rock me to sleep."

"Trains shake loose the houses," William said. "It's why the paint peels."

"Of course trains don't soothe the baby," Joe said. Last night Lauralee cried so hard and so long before she got the baby sling that Amee asked if Joe thought crying could kill her. The sobs sounded sometimes like choking.

"Babies don't like men," William told Joe. "Later she'll like you."

"Come on out, Amee," Joe said. "We'll hear her."

Amee leaned against the porch rail. "I've seen the sky lit before."

William glanced at Joe—she was being rude. Across the street ran ruptured rooflines and broken shingles she hadn't noticed when Joe first brought her here; "Sweet neighborhood," she'd said, still pregnant and dopey, not that she'd learned much since. If she was smart, she would be sleeping.

"It's a hundred years from now that I worry about." William spun the basketball in his hands. "These seeds coated with poison and the sun getting through holes. No stars, no quiet. It's fine for us but the kids should have better."

"They won't know a difference," Joe said.

"That's the problem with getting old. Knowing things. Better to stay dumb, Amee." He looked at her. "Don't pay attention to anything out here."

"I'm not dumb," she said. Joe looked at her, too.

"I meant it as a compliment," William said.

The amphitheater crooning stopped. The animals moaned on, less steady in volume and pitch, but deeper, sadder. She did feel like a child again. There was a bubble, only different things were inside it this time.

A red light flickered on the street: a high school kid on his bike. He wore a black sweatshirt and dark jeans and carried a backpack. Some parent let this kid leave the house blending into night; of course Amee's mother had barely noticed what she wore either.

He stopped in their driveway. "I brought milk." He dropped his backpack off his shoulder.

"I have milk," William told him. "It's not dementia. One time I forgot."

"Mom said to bring it."

William bounced the ball to Joe. The boy followed William across the street and his white sneakers sparked the pavement so that sadness cracked in Amee. She wanted to close her eyes and see a different picture. Joe stayed on the grass, passing the ball between his hands. A porch light came on down the street, spotlighting a rounded red door. Like it led to a fairytale.

"He's giving me a job," Joe said. "Admin assistant."

"Does he pay in world-weary platitudes? We could use more of those in our bank account."

"We'll find you a job next. Make friends. If it doesn't work, we'll move back to Omaha."

"I'm attached to this house. Don't you see it growing on my hip? It's not a complaint. My hips were never going to stay the same size."

Another train whistled, obscuring the wails again. Eight tracks through this town. A few blocks from here Amee had seen four trains running at the same time, but she only knew one kind that stopped—the one with the animals.

Joe leaned on the rail beside her. A cool breeze blew. "Last chance to see the purple sky."

"It isn't the last time. It isn't going back to black."

He nudged her waist with his hip. "One day when the whole sky's purple we'll say remember when it started? We lived in Nebraska."

A wail carried from the house. Rose in pitch, broke, repeated: the baby drowned out the train, the cows. Joe looked up like the porch roof was what cried. They went into the pocked-wood entryway, where warm air hung. Her old textbooks—Chemistry, Shakespeare, The History of the Civilized World—covered a stretch of exposed ductwork.

"Get ready for a long night." Amee pulled the sling's straps over her shoulders, the grooves in her skin.

"Let me tonight." Joe held the basketball in the crook of his arm.

"Next time." The sling felt light. The baby's cries crescendoed. Flies sprang from the stairs with each step. At first she'd wondered if she alone could hear the ghost train's lonely wails, but no: Joe had told her that they were cows, on their way to slaughter. Not lonely but scared, having spent their whole life in one small stall that stayed still, only to be forced in this other small stall that moved and stopped and those cows wondering when it would move again.

In the dark room, the baby's cries drowned out the town. Amee's body tensed but her chest ached for the sobs and shakes that would fall against it, the primitive metronome of a second heartbeat. She turned her face from her baby and listened.

# EXPANSION

THE HOUSE WAS FULL of old carpet and frayed wallpaper, not an original surface in sight (five bedrooms, three baths, 2500 square feet). Even the ceilings were wallpapered, seams visible. Kevin pointed them out to Julie.

"We'll get them painted," she said. "Everything needs to be painted."

"The bones are good," the realtor said. She was also their neighbor, an older woman who gave piano lessons to their six-year-old son. Probably she'd be happy to be rid of them as neighbors. Kevin mowed only when grass reached their shins. He left the recycling bin on the curb for days after pickup. Their sidewalks were cracked.

The realtor turned into the second bedroom and Kevin mumbled to Julie, "What about the spleen? The circulatory system?" Dusty air blew from vents.

"Be serious," Julie said. "It's double the space for barely any more money." She waddled down the red hallway (lumpy carpet, floral wallpaper) in her flared pregnancy shirt, hand on her abdomen. "For a house that hasn't been lived in for a year, it smells pretty good."

Her stomach seemed much larger than last time. He teased her about the waddling, but she seemed to like it, seemed already sentimental about losing it. The first two pregnancies she couldn't wait to get her body back. Now she was thirty-five years old and thirty-six weeks pregnant, hands always on her stomach; she talked about it as though fascinated by its size, its undulations, the bumps it sustained. Like she wanted to keep it.

The boys bounded past Kevin and into the room with Julie and the realtor. The youngest boy said, "What's that smell?" He was sobbing by the time Kevin entered. Something brown and crumpled lay in the corner. The realtor had disappeared. Julie frowned near a peeling window.

"Old houses get bats," she said. "We'll line the roof with wooden owls."

Kevin walked toward the animal with an urge to pick it up, see how big it was, if it just ate, if it was female, if it was pregnant. He wanted to see the shape of its teeth. But something about the way it lay crumpled like a thrown glove—he didn't want his kids near it. "You know which house doesn't have bats?" Kevin asked, lifting his sobbing son into his arms.

"It's a shoebox. I bump into everything."

"Another month and you lose the appendage." He held his son against his stomach, feeling the weight of his own "sympathy pounds" as Julie called them, like Kevin's body was preparing him for the extra space his family would soon collectively consume.

"Then it's the baby bumping into things," Julie said. "We need room to spread out."

"Don't touch it," Kevin told his oldest son, who stood an inch from the bat. He'd taught his kids about animal lifecycles, how not to fear dead things or feel sorry for them. Taxidermied animals filled his office; his freshman biology class dissected clams, crayfish, frogs. But those animals had been washed with chemicals, treated for study. He imagined this bat hurling itself into windows and walls, unable to find the vent it came through, dying in desperate attempt to escape.

The realtor returned with a broom and dustbin. "Most bats don't carry diseases," she said. "It's a myth they're all rabid."

"We're biologists," Julie said. "But we don't want them flying over our beds."

Kevin carried his son to the window so he wouldn't see the animal's disposal. Outside, a teenager with magenta hair and a cigarette rode by on a skateboard. She wore a tight shirt and cutoffs; her board's wheels scraped the pavement. It was obscene, her stick limbs and beautiful skin. Years ago Kevin had been friends with people like her; his longboard still hung in the shed. Now he would have liked to take the cigarette from her mouth, present a sweater, knee pads, long pants. He watched the girl and her knees turn the corner. Behind him, Julie rubbed her stomach.

"It needs some work," Julie told the realtor.

"Remember the bones," she said, hurrying away with the dustbin.

You're not supposed to make big purchases while pregnant, despite some impulse that sent millions of young parents fluttering in search of more twigs and twine. Julie had mocked such parents along with him through her first two pregnancies, so this time when he questioned rationally if they couldn't make their Prius work at least a few more years, he expected a shrug and a "Why not?" After all, Toyota's website listed several car seats small enough that a smart, economical family could fit three children across the backseat.

But everything was larger in this pregnancy. They rode home from the bat house in their new minivan, the four of them and their inflated feelings, though Julie hadn't driven the van since failing three times to maneuver into a grocery store parking spot. They'd had to switch in the middle so Kevin could park it. She claimed her stomach got in the way; she couldn't come close enough to the steering wheel. She preferred directing him from the passenger seat.

Kevin pulled up to their Tudor (three bedrooms, one bath, 1300 square feet) with its red door and ivy crawling up the side. The vines were overgrown; the rose bush's lower branches lay splayed on the ground as though beaten with something heavy. But he loved this house. When they'd first viewed it six years ago, Julie had carried their first baby up the porch steps and peered through the doorway, enthralled. She said it looked like a dollhouse, something in a fairytale. Now that they considered giving it up, Kevin saw it this way again: a tiny place to cram their life into, squeeze into every corner books and pieces of furniture, toys that were small but not choking hazards. His family would keep growing, expanding to fill the miniature hallways; they'd bump into each other at the dinner table like helium balloons, smiling and contained.

"This is a solid house," Kevin said in the entryway (vaulted ceiling, oak floors). "No bats or birds or rodents." The boys kicked off their shoes and went running. Julie picked up the boys' shoes; every time she bent over, she grunted. She shoved the shoes into Kevin's arms and gave him a look like this is why they needed to move. The boys' footsteps echoed above their heads.

"It'd be more space to make a mess of," he said. He put the shoes in the closet crammed with coats and boots and vacuum. In the storage bench by the door he dropped the hats and sunscreen they'd left in a heap the day before. The boys shrieked above them, and Julie shook her head at the ceiling. She straightened the mail on the console table.

"I want to make a mess," she said. "Whole rooms can be designated and we'll lock them shut when guests visit."

She sat on the bench and lifted her feet, glanced at him miserably. Like every day for the past three months, Kevin sat on the rug and made himself take off her shoes. Her feet were swollen, purplish in places, and sweaty. They felt like dead animals in his hands: foreign in size and shape from what they'd been when living. He rubbed them and she sighed, gazing vaguely at the wall behind him like it was a magic picture: molecules that would split open and show her the bones.

"You're just tired," he said weakly.

Julie put her hands on her stomach. "It's too tight," she said. "Everything's about to explode." She splayed her fingers across her abdomen like she carried the world. "Baby's moving," she said peacefully, her gaze moving inward. He wanted to feel the size and shape of what lay inside, trace the still-soft bones while the baby stayed small within its small world. But his hands seemed thick and dangerous. He couldn't stop the swelling.

*"Life is always a rich and steady time when you are waiting for something to hatch."*
—E.B. White, *Charlotte's Web*

PEOPLE CHEER A PREGNANT woman running, a thick support band beneath her belly and a slow steady pace like a moving habitat, a thriving biome on this paved Nebraska path. She lumbers past prairie grass, over roads, beneath a train overpass, around a lake. "Superwoman!" people yell as they pass by. "Keep going!" The sky is blue and shining. But her legs hurt, everything's stretched too tight and even small muscles she doesn't have names for swell. She suspects no one will cheer for her once the baby's born, when she's no longer her own ecosystem but a lone planet with a ring of flesh loose around its middle.

Knowing what to expect, she can enjoy things that took her by surprise the first and second pregnancies. The tremoring of the body like an earthquake coming, the geysers in the throat that force her to sleep upright and tilted—she is an anthropologist studying the rhythms of these pressures that will come and go like a season. The third baby is something extra she's sneaking in before her body won't support it anymore. If she tilts her mind a certain way she can convince herself she isn't really pregnant, like in the middle of a run when her mind finds peace as the body churns on.

Part of the pleasure is having someone to suffer in front of. Her stomach proceeds her like a flag. She leans back (to accommodate the bulk), juts it (to ease her aching hips), presses it against her husband's back in the small bathroom (am I crowding *you?*). Her stomach grows smooth and tight, and at night she covers it in cream so slick her shirt sticks like plastic wrap. This amazing body! It stretches! It endures! Her husband hears her litany of cramps, given-up foods, ingenious maneuvers to perform simple tasks. They watch her stomach. Even beneath the covers her objective swells.

But she's ready to get on with it: the red-faced alien crying before the milk comes in; the raw pinching of first nursing; the merging of sleep with the baby: two hours on, two off. That morning, in bed, she presses stomach lumps that must be legs or elbows and sees through the window new leaves on branches. She reads to her older children, walks with her husband, runs—enjoy these things! Restaurants, auditoriums, a bright sunlit street midday. She wants the small body in her arms.

Maybe it's another level of martyrdom she's after. When her husband tells people she's still running at nine months pregnant ("Five miles! Four times a week!") he shakes his head amazed. Their friends are also amazed but make comments like "that's crazy," and she senses her husband is a bit mocking, even bitter. Like she's overdoing it with the nobility and self-discipline. Like he'd feel better if she were on the couch, legs on pillows and a cake on her stomach. *Be a normal human!* is the subtext of his bragging. *Let yourself go; gain some weight; enough already!* Her legs, the traitors, agree with him; soon three miles is all she can handle, then two, so slow and steady like she's swelled to her edges—sluggish now, rolling, looking for a place to settle. She runs two miles, stops, stretches her tight tight legs, then tries for another half; her lungs are fine, everything's fine, only her legs so weak under this weight. She isn't ready to be a planet. She wants her husband's admiration even if he resents her for it.

She sees them everywhere. Babies in tight cotton wraps against people's chests. Babies with unsteady heads in shopping carts. Babies riding on people's waists; lifting themselves on fat wobbling legs. Babies in portable car seats straining against straps to see something behind them. Babies suddenly still, listening.

This woman belongs to history and myth: the bearer of life, fruit of humanity. What it must feel like to be an object admired, not human, though it breathes, it moves, amazing! At the store, the school, the university where she works, on the bike/run path, this woman gazes ahead as people approach her habitat. Even alone with the mirror who she sees is not really her, but HER. She feigns obliviousness to avoid conceit; anyway it is temporary, and loose flesh looms.

A mother craves the future even as her ecosystem unravels. Pregnancy's wholeness gives to the closeness of nursing gives to a toddler good and heavy in a lap until he struggles from her arms, runs across the room, across the lawn, down the street, to college in a different state, and then to his own family, where he'll start a new ecosystem she has to travel further and further to reach. The weight of the future is its own habitat, threatening descent on the one that's growing.

Still, part of the pleasure is looking forward to the ending. Breath returning to normal, rediscovering her own steady pace. She's spent months watching this stomach jut impossibly beneath her hands, and suddenly it will be gone. Not a loss, really; she'll have the baby and sleep on her back and eat pizza. She'll tell herself the regaining of her body is nearly as interesting as pregnancy, the fleshy aftermath sagging around her like a burst soufflé. It will hang around for two full years. But when the evidence is gone and the body's just a body, skin and bones and muscles moving to move, she won't think about it, she won't even notice it, except when she misses the weight, and the company.

# SEATTLE

MY BROTHER AND HIS girlfriend are on their way to "The mythical land of Seattle." This is what they call it. They are broke, jobless. They hold hands in my sunlit living room. "It's really expensive there," my husband says. "And you don't have jobs?" My kids crowd around my legs, say hello in their nice clothes, answer questions like little yes-no adults. "Jobs aren't everything," my brother says, smiling at the kids, impressed. "Just wait," I say.

A paradise of restaurants, shops, and galleries. Down their crammed street, if they find a cross street, they will see mountains. I live in the middle of Nebraska. They're visiting me on their way West. Their fifteen-foot truck parked in our driveway, their guitar, banjo, and bags piled in the room where diapers are usually changed, wooden toys chewed on, board books happily dismantled. "There's also the ocean," my brother says. "Cold and shining."

My kids drop toys at my brother and his girlfriend's feet like cats drop dead mice. They clomp on the piano and look back for applause; they try forks at dinner. My husband serves organic everything. My brother and his girlfriend have eaten only peanut butter sandwiches and crackers for the last two days.

While my husband and I wash dishes, my brother and his girlfriend read to the kids on our couch, the windows dark but the house full and brimming with light.

The scene shatters with kids prodded upstairs, stripped naked and let loose shrieking down the hall, wrenched from baths, hair detangled, clothes chosen, diapers changed, books closed, songs ended, heads coaxed toward darkness, screams, legs rushing at crib bars, pacifiers found, more screams. My husband and I come down darkened stairs an hour later to my brother and his girlfriend holding hands on the couch. The room is eerily peaceful with only one light burning, like they've reversed the house's charge by detaching from its currents. My husband admits, yes, every night is like this. I say, "I hope a couple days with us won't turn you off having kids." My brother says, "Don't worry. We were pretty sure we didn't want them already."

In the morning my oldest practices cello. My brother and his girlfriend come sleepy-eyed downstairs, intertwine on the couch and watch this novelty. The younger two kids leap around the room like lumbering pixies. I've read how your brain changes when you have kids: empathy grows, ambition shrinks, but maybe it's just asset collection, like the women in the Target parking lot with long trails of children. I want to be a duck with ducklings, too.

My brother and his girlfriend nod encouragingly at the coffee shop I later bring them to: Wow, a coffee shop in Nebraska! They are going to the Land of Coffee Shops. I buy their coffee because they have no money, but being poor doesn't bother them when they soon will stroll hand-in-hand down Seattle sidewalks. How could they have kids when there are too many people in this world already? They sip coffee, look out the window at dusty grass and train tracks. Not to mention they want to enjoy each other, do adult things like drink wine and go to art galleries. I tell them, "Your kids will be the kind of people the world could use more of." Their one-bedroom apartment will cost more than my mortgage. They will bus to museums on first Thursdays of the month because they can get in free. My brother tells me, "This is a good place for you right now. It doesn't have to be exciting."

That afternoon my kids are curious about the guitar and banjo on their way to Seattle, but my brother and his girlfriend want to do kid-things: walk to the park barefoot and spin through grass. There are things to see in Nebraska. These fields that start flat and green and pliable and grow tall and yellow and stiff. How can people not want them? This tangle of dirty feet in the entryway, the wet spots on the carpet, the doorways they stand in with questions, the chocolate they pilfer and eat in the bathroom, the floor they lay on screaming, the sprinklers they see on and the muddy yard they sprint for without even hesitating.

Off Seattle's coast are dozens of islands to explore. I imagine my brother and his girlfriend ferrying from shore to shore, happy to move between separate things, and I want my mind to stretch there with them, to feel what it is they want. That night while everyone sleeps, I google pictures of rocky shorelines and lush green paths. In the pictures the sky is blue, even though everyone knows Seattle's sky holds more gray shades than my kids' murky paint water. But I can't even tell them what everyone says—that love, that purpose, that when you're old, that you will regret not. The sun shines most days in Nebraska. It's watching and seeing in a different way. It's not-excitement that can define a life, and where are your wits if you can't survive a few sleepless nights?

The next morning, I hug my brother and his girlfriend. Give them a grocery bag I've emptied my pantry into. The couch sags in the living room, and I see how quickly they've become part of the sum and how unprepared I am for this emptying. I take the big kids to school and when I get home, the truck's gone, the curb as white as it always is. I send my mind out with them, driving further west than I've been. My youngest squirms in my arms and I lower her onto the big, shining lawn, and feel like a coast chasing an island.

*"We keep moving forward, opening new doors…curiosity keeps leading us down new paths."*

— Walt Disney

AT DISNEY WORLD LAST summer, a guy loading trays of food onto a buffet line asked where I was from. I told him Nebraska, which was where I flew in from, though Alabama or North Carolina or Michigan could've been just as accurate; home is a floating X as you leave places, as you move on. We were in the Tusker House, a restaurant in the Animal Kingdom themed after an African Marketplace, a dozen tables spread with pickled vegetables, curries, chickpea salads, hummus, seasoned meats, miniature desserts. While you ate, Donald, Mickey, and Goofy, all in Safari clothes, visited your table to hop, nod, and gesture mutely. The guy was young, friendly. He told me I looked like someone he met working for Ringling Brothers, but I'd never been in the circus, and he knew the girl he met wasn't from Nebraska. I juggled plates for me and two of my children. He asked if I liked living in Nebraska, and I shrugged. "It's easy." "Yeah," he said, "living there, you probably like coming here and seeing some things. To someone like me, surrounded by this, it sounds pretty nice to go somewhere with nothing around." This made me feel better about living where I lived. Also guilty, because when I'm in Nebraska I complain about the flatness.

There are cities with more restaurants and culture, progressive schools for my kids, bigger houses. There is more money to be made elsewhere; I could be closer to my parents; I could live somewhere that is not *this place*, with the monotony and the ways I've embarrassed myself and the crazy wind always blowing trash in our yard. My husband and I have twice been offered jobs since moving to Nebraska, and though we haven't left, we still talk about it sometimes. We distract ourselves with work, house renovations, dinner parties, another baby. It's a desire for something new I have to weigh myself against.

I've given myself permission to go once a year. This seems reasonable. More often than that would be excessive; anyone who tells me they've gone two or three times in one year, I understand the temptation. It's an addiction, a coping mechanism. Talking about Disney, dreaming about Disney—it's easier than the news, than drugs, poverty, pollution, sickness, real people, real problems. Even if my trip is ten months away, getting through the day is easier knowing next summer I will stroll the immaculate Boardwalk, eat harissa chicken kabobs and mascarpone cheesecake with orange blossom honey ice cream beside elaborate topiaries, enter palaces, hear songs from bushes and fountains, immerse in fairyland after fairyland on boats and trams and trains and foot, an endless array of places to move into.

How long can I live in Nebraska and still say I'm not really from here? Five years, and I haven't gathered the place around me. Even people who live here ask how I ended up in Nebraska, smirk as though maybe I've been tricked. "It's fine," I say. "There isn't anything wrong with it." The same smirk from friends and family living in cliché-cool places like New York, Seattle, D.C. But logical things: routine, a flexible schedule. I can walk to work, walk downtown; there are several coffee shops, even a professional theater company. Sure I'm curious about the places I could live, places that could be terrible—population-dense places, cold places, huge places, conservative places, polluted places, high-crime places: the sheen of newness that obscures dark corners. Even cities I've previously lived in occupy bright parts of my mind like travel-brochure memories; I've let fade the gray days, the traffic, the fire ants, the hot hot sun or the black chunks of ice lining curbs all winter. Logical things.

I don't like to admit it to people. My husband or one of the kids bring it up, and people say, "Didn't you just go last year?" And I can't look at them, it's so indulgent and embarrassing. I feel sick thinking about the money. I tell myself experience is what counts in this life. I tell myself we work hard and deserve it. I tell myself it's for the kids. But no, it's unnecessary and it's for me. This year we will go with my husband's family, so I won't have to admit it's taken me over like a sickness. A family reunion! It doesn't matter our conversations will take place in lines and crowded restaurants, wrangling kids, applying sunscreen, fanning faces, buying things. How does it feel working in a place where each day thousands of people pass through? Never the same people, all these faces, bodies, gestures. Every worker must be on the lookout for people who remind them of people from their past: they must be vigilant for this, subconsciously, to feel less burdened by this swollen population. These people they must serve, all of them wealthy *enough*, some obscenely rich, fanning themselves, eating chocolate bananas, moving to the next attraction. And I get why families of twenty or thirty come all wearing the same red or white or black shirt with their Family Name + Disney Vacation 20__! blazoned across the front. Comforted in a sea of consumption to see a few people they know.

Hundreds of tunnels run beneath the Magic Kingdom. This is where the trash disappears to, magically, and how they make deliveries. Costumed characters walk the "utilidors" to move between locations without dissonance, so you don't see, say, Buzz Lightyear in the same Land as Cinderella. There is a restaurant at the Magic Kingdom that serves Thanksgiving Dinner two times a day, every day. People who work at Disney are called "cast members." We take the Contemporary Resort boat around a huge lake connecting several other resorts. I ask the guy steering the boat how he's doing. "Good!" he says. "Only three more rounds this shift." He says this exuberantly. It isn't his tone that makes reality pulse the edges of my vacation—here's a person who may not enjoy every minute of his job, nothing shocking about this, except it does shock me, when I'm here, immersed in candy coating. These are the moments I want to take home with me, when the façade breaks and I see people who are as sick of where they are as I am. Or worse. The whole boat ride across the wide blue lake, I do the math: in an eight hour shift he goes forty times around this water, repeating the same enthusiastic lines about where we're headed and how people should keep from falling off, or injuring themselves. Don't forget: time's only valuable if there's somewhere else you want to be.

There are reasons. A country, a state, a city. Here in the middle's where I live. Low crime, modest income gap, decent places to work—a regional University, Buckle Headquarters, several tech startups—and everyone more comfortable in jeans and sweatshirts than heels and makeup. There are doors I could walk through. I'm a little curious. But logical things. Lists. The new place could be worse. I won't like my job, the house will be too big, the walk to work longer, the weather colder, the kids moodier, and I can see that I'm part of the problem. I'm not as scrappy as I used to be. And the clean green parks. Prairie grass feathers and the huge sky. The ground is firm and flat. The sun comes out nearly every day.

It was unnecessary for him to speak to me. He stood on the other side of the African buffet, the glass shield angled between us. He bent low to see me straight on. He had finished loading food; I wasn't the girl from the circus. Was lingering required, part of the show? Part of this illusion that wealthy-ish people dreamt about, paid for, entered, and took home with them. What happens behind the curtains, the doors and roped areas marked "cast members only"? Beneath the ground that feels solid but is actually a city submerged in concrete—gray walls, gray sky—where you'll find Mickey and Pluto crossing paths with merchandise carts and garbage trucks? How many insights does this guy hand vacationers a night? Because he didn't smirk at Nebraska. And I looked like a girl he used to know. At a certain angle, he said, a flat landscape can be the most appealing thing in the world.

Because for so long, *struggle* and nothing to do but want—more money, more years, a degree, a job, a house, a roof that doesn't leak, some things published, a bank account that doesn't shrink, more children, more sleep, more money, more organic, my body back in shape, new windows, new carpet, more time. Then to realize: plenty of money, a fine house, the kids off to school, time to work and write and exercise and think. An abundance of everything. Stunned, I look around at people still struggling, struggling more than I ever did. And what can I do? Send donation checks, argue politics, feel guilty about it. Thrash about for new ways to suffer, new things to want, some blinding, vital ambition. Book another trip to Disney.

Bringing my kids to Epcot's miniature world, I have to tell them the real Eiffel Tower is much much bigger, and those totem poles in "Canada" are kind of offensive, and the "three amigos" do not bounce around the real Mexico City, which is also not entirely full of balloons, dancing women and guitar-strumming, mustached, floral-shirt-wearing men. Disney doesn't acknowledge Germany's complicated history, or China's—of course not!—it doesn't show the poverty, the wars, the people slogging through rain or snow or heat to jobs, burdened by cancer and eviction, death of loved ones, divorce. But I stroll the "British" gardens and my kids dance at the "German" restaurant; we watch the "Chinese Acrobats" and eat sushi on plastic plates. Maybe I can't handle the gray grit of a real city, even as I crave chaos, noise and light. There are so many doorways at Disney! Fireworks! Dancing animals! Everyone smiling, flowers blooming, every step of it safe and polished and bright.

## Author Note

---

JESSICA HOLLANDER is the author of the story collection *In These Times the Home is a Tired Place*, which won the Katherine Anne Porter Prize. She has published in many journals such as *The Georgia Review*, *The Gettysburg Review*, *The Cincinnati Review*, *The Journal*, *Quarterly West*, *Hayden's Ferry Review*, and *Sonora Review*. She received her MFA from the University of Alabama and is now an Associate Professor at the University of Nebraska at Kearney.